Baby Honu's Incredible Journey

Written & Illustrated by Tammy Yee

ISLAND HERITAGE

Produced, published and distributed by
Island Heritage
First Edition, Thirty-Eighth Printing, 2015
ISBN No. 0-89610-285-8
COP 140411

Address orders and editorial correspondence to:

ISLAND HERITAGE
A DIVISION OF THE MADDEN CORPORATION
94-411 KO'AKI STREET
WAIPAHU, HAWAI'I 96797-2806
Orders: (800) 468-2800 Info: (808) 564-8800
Fax: (808) 564-8877 www.islandheritage.com

To Ric, Cosmo and Dylan~
Thank you for your love, patience and support.

T.Y.

One warm August night, beneath a full summer moon, Mother Honu came ashore.

She searched the beach and found a bright patch of sand safely beyond the high tide's hungry reach.

"This will be the perfect nursery for my babies," she thought.

Then she set to work, scraping a sandy nest beside the blooming naupaka. She dug and she dug. It was hard work, and she labored through the night.

When the nest was deep enough, Mother Honu laid her eggs. Into the hole they gently tumbled, one hundred eggs in all! When she was finished, she lovingly covered her clutch with sand. Then she carefully smoothed the sand over with her wide, flat belly.

With her babies safely hidden, Mother Honu crawled back to the ocean's edge. "Goodbye, little ones," she whispered softly as she slipped beneath the waves.

Deep within the nest, in the comfort of his egg, Baby Honu slept. And as he slept, he dreamt. He had wonderful dreams, magical dreams, of splendid creatures afloat in starry seas.

Baby Honu grew and grew.

One evening, Baby Honu was wakened by a busy stirring within the nest. All around him, his brothers and sisters were pushing and stretching. The little turtles poked and prodded and kicked and shoved at one another.

9

The time had come to leave their cozy eggs. One by one, the little turtles broke free of their leathery eggshells. Slowly, they made their way to the surface of their sandy nest.

Pop! Pop! Pop! Out they popped! Out into the big, wide world!

Baby Honu looked about. Where were the great floating creatures that he had dreamt about? Where was the sea? Wide-eyed, he dillydallied beneath the naupaka as his brothers and sisters raced toward the moonlit water.

By the time he ventured out onto the beach, the moon had begun to set. Dawn was coming. Baby Honu hurried, his flippers flapping clumsily in the sand.

Near the shore, the hungry ʻōhiki waited. They crouched on spindly legs, guarding the entrances to their burrows with their terrible claws. Patiently they waited as the baby turtles approached.

As Baby Honu scampered toward the sea, a huge 'ōhiki burst from its burrow and chased after him. Poor Baby Honu! Try as he might, he could not scurry any faster! 'Ōhiki came nearer and nearer, his angry claw snapping wildly in the air.

Just then, Baby Honu stumbled over a strand of pōhuehue. Over and over he tumbled, away from ʻŌhiki and under a large pōhuehue leaf. There he hid, as ʻŌhiki searched for him.

13

14

'Ōhiki searched and searched, but could not find the little turtle. The large crab returned to his burrow to wait for easier prey. For now, Baby Honu was safe.

Baby Honu cowered beneath the leaf. In his egg, he was safe and warm. In his egg, there were no terrible crabs, waiting to gobble him up! Where was the sea that his dreams had promised?

In the shade of the pōhuehue, cradled by cool, green leaves and lavender blossoms, Baby Honu thought about returning to his egg and going back to sleep.

Instead, he felt soft prodding at his side. It was his sister.

"Hurry, we must go to the sea," she whispered.

"But I can't," cried Baby Honu, covering his head with his flippers. He was so afraid. How could he ever leave the safety of the pōhuehue?

"Come with me," said his sister tenderly. "We'll be safe in the sea. We can go together."

And together they crawled out from beneath the leaf...

...and hurried after their brothers and sisters as they dashed toward the waiting sea.

Suddenly, a large shadow swept over Baby Honu. Out from the sky plunged a large 'Iwa, his magnificent black wings blocking out the early morning sun.

18

"Got you!" screeched
'Iwa as he snatched the little turtle in
his claws. Baby Honu's sister watched
fearfully as he was carried up and away.
Up and away from the beach. Up and
away from his brothers and sisters. Baby
Honu could feel the rush of air from
'Iwa's powerful wings as he was carried
higher and higher. He struggled to free
himself from the bird's grasp, but the
bird was much too strong.

'Iwa soared high above the beach and out over the ocean.

The giant bird was just about to gulp him down when a large, red-footed booby swooped by, his belly full of fish.

A belly full of fish! Now, if there's one thing that an impy 'iwa cannot resist, it is to bully another bird into releasing his breakfast. Suddenly, Baby Honu did not look so tasty after all.

'Iwa dropped the little turtle and with a loud whoop, flapped after the booby.

Baby Honu fell through the air, down to the sea. Wildly, he flapped his flippers, but still he fell. Down, down, down, he plummeted.

Plop! Instead of falling into the sea as he had hoped, he fell onto something hard. And big. And black. What was this strange island afloat within the sea?

Baby Honu explored the wet, barnacled surface. Suddenly the ground swelled beneath him. A great tower of water and mist exploded from a nearby hole.

A Koholā! Baby Honu had landed upon a mighty Koholā!

The noble giant swam on, oblivious to its tiny passenger.

From atop Koholā's broad back, Baby Honu could see the world. The ocean was big and beautiful and blue, just as he had dreamt it to be. All around him, mālolo burst from the water and sailed through the air.

Below him swam a shimmering school of squid. The water bubbled and churned as seabirds dropped from the sky and plunged after the fish and squid.

On they sailed, Baby Honu and Koholā.

F inally, Koholā dove beneath the waves. Baby Honu watched as the majestic whale descended into the depths. Koholā had let him off in a gentle ocean current. Ghostly jellyfish and tangled seaweed drifted by.

Ahead of him, Baby Honu could see tiny specks afloat within the current. As he swam nearer, he could see that the tiny specks were tiny sea turtles. His family! Baby Honu had finally found his family!

Baby Honu's sister eagerly swam up to him and gave him a great big turtle hug. Soon, he was surrounded by joyous little turtles playfully diving, twisting, and circling about him.

Baby Honu's incredible journey was over. He was once again with his brothers and sisters, in the safety of the open sea. The ocean and its great creatures were every bit as wondrous as he had dreamt them to be.

Glossary of Hawaiian Words

Honu - The Pacific Green Sea Turtle is a threatened marine turtle that breeds and nests in the remote Northwestern Hawaiian Islands. These gentle giants can grow up to four feet long and weigh up to 400 pounds. They can be seen swimming gracefully near the shoreline, grazing on seaweed.

'Iwa - The Hawaiians call the Great Frigatebird 'Iwa, which means "thief." 'Iwa often bully other birds into releasing their catch, which the 'Iwa then "steals" as its own. 'Iwa are superb flyers. They soar majestically over coastal waters, and can be recognized by their long, slender wings and forked tails.

Koholā - Humpback Whales arrive in Hawai'i each winter to mate and calve, and return to Alaska each summer to feed on krill and small schooling fish. Mothers and calves can sometimes be seen playfully jumping and rolling in deep waters off Moloka'i, Lāna'i, Kaho'olawe, and Maui.

Mālolo - Flying fish

Naupaka - A hardy coastal shrub common on Hawaiian beaches

'Ōhiki - Ghost crab

Pōhuehue - Seaside Morning Glory